# ELYSIUM ABYSS

YIJIA LIN

2022

Elysium Abyss



ISBN: 9798844504310

*To 8Z*
*always n forever*

# CONTENTS

# PART A

# ONE

**SOMETHING WAS PULLING ME TOWARDS THE BUILDING.**

I heard a scream - it was inevitable.
The gate opened itself.
One step.
Two steps.
Three steps.
One more, and I'm close to death.
Will I put it off?
The voice from behind answered my question.
"Do it."
I grabbed the knife and headed towards the girl in the corner. There was nothing in the way to thwart me now.
She was terrified and looked kind of familiar. As I lifted my knife and ready to stab.
"NO!"
I found myself screaming as I woke up.
Nightmares. Again.

Everything gave me a strong de ja vu, it was like

I've been there before, and possibly lived there for a really long time…who am I, you might ask? My name is Alexia Lively. Age 17, junior at St.Clarke's.

Oh and by the way, I'm an arsonist. What do I mean by that? Well, I certainly do have little knowledge of my family. My brother, Dylan and my sister, Claudia along with 5-year-old me burned the house we lived in with our father, Vladimir in it alive. He was an obdurate tyrant to the society, all of us did what we think was plausible, and I guess the three of us were all libertarians. We rescued our mother hastily, Adriana, when we realized that we made a mistake.

We needed to get away while we watched our house got blighted and plummet to the ground.

We enshrouded from the society.

So here we go, having the scene where we ran and ran and ran and ran, disguising ourselves as much as possible to try and cover up our reprehensible mistake.

A rotten tunnel became our shelter for the next fourteen nights. And the  next day, I found myself magically on an actual bed facing a plain ceiling. Claudia and Dylan's beds were beside mine. The building that we were in was capacious and it was like a conventional bedroom ornate with flowers.

"Oh hey, you woke up." Said a woman who looked to be a 20-year-old beside my bed.


I eschewed her stare. She was red-headed with two braids, a pair of jeans, a black t-shirt that says I.O at the front, hoop earrings, sunglasses, gray eyes, small nose, and a curvy lip without any additional makeup besides having a bit of pink on her lips.

"Where's mom?" I asked her precipitously, but she ignored me.

"My name is Cheryl Coleman, I will be you three's life coach." She said, smiling, "You are in the headquarter of our society. You have nothing to worry about and we will protect you against any deleterious thing that might came in the way of you three for burning your house."

"So..child protection services?"

Claudia asked her tentatively.

"Pretty much."

"Are you some spy that the government sends to lynch criminals? Cause I'm pretty sure we are all arsonists now." Said Dylan, frowning.

Cheryl chuckled and enunciated her speech, "Let me break it down for you, we are..." I knew she was equivocating, but she continued, "..specialists to shield kids that err. I'm sure none of you kids are blunderbusses."

"Where do we live now? Here? We don't have anywhere else to go. All of us were impecunious." Claudia asked her ludicrously, like that was going to help us leave this place.

"Good news, the headquarter already provides you three and your mother a place to live. Your mother is already there, she needed the rest. We put the three of you in shirts that can be less conspicuous to the outside." Said Cheryl lucidly.

I looked around. Dylan, Claudia and I were wearing the same black shirt that says I.O at the front, also jeans, sneakers with an extra black leather jacket. The three of us heeded this woman, as we had nothing else better to do besides acquiesce in presence her.

"Great, now we are going full Dylan." Claudia murmured and lampooned Dylan's bland facial expression.

[…]

A few years later, mom died of cancer and it hit us hard. I was 7 then.

However, the tragedies never stopped and they happened practically once in  a while. Probably it was the most reasonable punishment that the one from above could give us…me, specifically, to regret and reflect on my transgression.

"I'm so sorry, Alexia." Said Cheryl after she broke out of her usual poised status, crying, "They are both gone."

My life completely turned around with the arcane murder of my brother, Dylan Lively being stabbed in the heart by a man named X as we call him. He was 19. This enigmatic man made hatred his most useful weapon and engendered a scene with my sister, Claudia Lively. As far as I can tell, when she went to carry out her revenge, she tripped and fell off of a ferris wheel. She died at the age of 18.

There were no therapeutic attempts to cure me from tragedies. No analgesic seemed to work. I was trapped in an emotional maelstrom that keeps spinning incessantly.

Sometimes my head spins so fast and it would get deteriorated every single day. I wish panacea could palliative me, but there was no such thing.

I will never be able to approach a ferris wheel or like the letter x.

Ever

Again.

# TWO

**I LIVED WITH CHERYL EVER SINCE.**

"Come on, girl. You are going to be late, hurry up!"

"Alright, alright, I'll be down in a minute. I don't know why you are so worried about me being late."

"Um…it's not good for your personal record…?"

I laughed and rushed to the white Ferrari at the front porch, sat at the back as Cheryl took the driver's seat.

"I still don't get why I'm in a boarding school and I have to come home every weekend." I showed my bristle while she pulled out her car.

Cheryl drove fast enough to make the Sunday 8pm deadline for my dorm parent, and she left without saying goodbye.

"Hey Alexia, just on time."

"How do you do, Ms. Andrews?"

"Please, it's Lana." She smiled, "Ms. Cooper is waiting for you." "ALEXIA!" Shouted the blonde who had distinct facial features with green eyes, peaking behind the ajar door.

I hugged her. That is my roommate and my best friend, Carly Cooper.  A school skirt, a school shirt, a tie, and a pair of boots, it was classic her.

"Ready for
tomorrow?" She
asked,
interested.
"Not at all…"
"We are going to be awesome this year then."

[…]

It was the first week of school.

Concord wasn't exactly the perfect place to… live. It was an archaic county. New Hampshire was too frigid and it snowed too often. Though one of the perks was that we would get random days off so arbitrary that we would just stay at home for the week. We were excited at first, but it became banal as time passed.

First weeks were always the hardest— One of the newbies hooked up with a popular senior, the teacher bribed the principal to get the job, some depressed weirdos got beat up by the mob, the lunch lady was pregnant, one of the cheerleaders became fat and got kicked off the team, or some kids turned a casual conversation into an epic forbidden romance. But the most important of them all, picture day. Big deal, big deal. Nobody wanted to be ashamed of themselves 50 years later when they show their yearbook to their grandchildren. So much for peaking in high school.

However, it was the first Wednesday of

September. The day before picture day when I heard that Madison Parker, captain of the girls varsity swimming team went missing. I was on the same team with her last year. We got close for a week, and then she went ahead and dumped me for the girl who brought her concert tickets to 5 Seconds of Winter or something. I've been obviating her ever since. The coach said she called in sick when we had our practice on Wednesday. However, she did not show up the following week, nor the week after that.

And that's when it hit me.

She's defunct.

How do I know?

Ever heard of the expression, "if the victim cannot be found by the police within the next three days, she's either going to be dead, or doesn't want to be found." I had a strong hunch about the first option.

For the following weeks, the Concord police had done everything that they could to try and find her body, but there was no clue. The kids at school last saw her on Tuesday, in gym class. Her close friends said that she told them her head hurt, and she went to the nurse for treatment, but the school nurse never even saw her there on Tuesday.

The adults told us that she was running away from home and she would come back soon. Nobody believed them—something else might also be going on and no one else has a clue.

Cheryl would call and check on me every single day for security. Her exact words are "Is the school safe right now? Should I come pick you up? Should I let the headquarters give you a mission so you can ditch school right now? " Carly would laugh so hard whenever she heard Cheryl on the phone, giving me a hyperbole as like she always do. Carly would indicate her as a sister who tries so hard to be a mother but failed. I couldn't argue 'cause she got that right.

In the following week, the school interrogated every single one of the students and that included me and Carly.

"You were on the same varsity swimming team as Ms. Parker, correct?"

"Yes…sir."

"Were you two close?"

"Not really."

"Mind if you explain that?"

"We were for a week, then we were not because she became best friends with Rebecca since she brought her concert tickets."

"Do you guys have any other interactions for the following week or after that?"

"Just the swim team. I see her for practice. Nothing else."

"Noted. Thank you for your cooperation."

The Concord county finally got their clues of their precious swim team captain in the following week. Madison committed suicide. And…

**IT'S ALL YOUR FAULT.**

Was the first thing that I saw when I went back to my dorm. Capitalized, in Madison's handwriting. Big and bold imprinted on my wall above my bed. The posters on the wall were ripped off. Tapes that were there to hold the posters got scraped, nothing was left. Except those four words.

I found myself screaming in the center of my double.

The Concord police were gathered behind me, the room was spinning. My head went blank.

"Ms.Lively, we are so sorry, Claudia and Dylan were gone. May they rest in peace."

The county police assembled at our house.

Cheryl and I buried both of their bodies at the cemetery behind our backyard.

"Ms.Lively? Ms.Lively? Are you listening?" Said Sheriff Keller in front of me, "I am aware that your family members are gone. Could that be a motive that you bullied Madison to death?"

I looked at his affable face, "You think I bullied her to death?"

"Well, according to the handwriting on the wall, it's the most possible reason. But please elaborate on what happened between you two? More specifics this time please, would you?"

"I told you, we were only friends for a week, less than a week perhaps. She did come up to me and wished me good luck for picture day on Tuesday's gym class."

The sheriff wrote my words down, "Are these her normal behaviors?" "Everyone wishes each other good luck before picture day. It's a St. Clarke's thing. No big deal."

"Noted. Now, as you mentioned before, did she ever tell you when or why did she went to the 5SOS concert or who she went with?"

"She did solicit me to come along with her

the night before the concert, I was not feeling well that night, so she went with Rebecca."

"Why were you not feeling well then? Headache?"

"Yes. I drank too much water."

"Does drinking water often hurt your health?"

"Yes, it makes my head twirl." I paused, seeing him frown, "It's true. Ask Cheryl if you don't believe me."

"Alright, Ms.Lively, you are not under arrest then. Keep up the good work at school. Don't ditch." He smiled.

"Thanks." I murmured.

The following week, which was the last week of September, people were talking. Apparently I'm the jinx, and they say Madison was going to haunt me posthumously. Carly didn't mind. She kept on telling me not to worry about it. I told Cheryl what happened, she said she was just sorry that it happened to me again. I personally don't mind the name callings and the rumors, those were all stupid. I can hold on to everything as long as I have Cheryl and Carly.

I always like them better than I seemed to.

# THREE

**BY OCTOBER, EVERYTHING WAS EXACERBATED BY THE DEATH OF MADISON.**

Apparently St.Clarke's was covered in the shadow of Madison's death. The school was taking their chances to expand homework load with alacrity. Advocative posters were everywhere on the wall. Sports practices went from two hours to 2.5 hours. More inspections came, one before 8am, one after  dinner and one right before lights out. Just to prevent kids from doing drugs and they made our limited two hours study hall to one hour for squeezing an hour of therapy. And of course, the others censured me for the loss of everything.

For the first week, the entire grade went out for a trip. Our biology teacher, Mr. Anderson said it could take our mind off all the dark stuff. I never fully understood that man, but It was nice to go out though. However, very unfortunately, he took us to an amusement park. Carly headed to the carousel directly. I told her she should go ahead without me while I found myself standing and gazing at the ferris wheel weirdly.

"Alexia." Said the voice behind me that sounded kind of distant but familiar.

"Claudia?" I realized I was looking at my dead sister standing behind me, "Are you real? You look the same but…a bit rotund kind of way?"

"Of course I'm not, silly." She put her arms around me, I almost felt her, "I'm just your imaginations, and thanks for the compliment, but I want you to deliberate why am I here. "

"I mean…you looked so real." I said while ruminating about her presence, "Can I touch you? Whoah, my subconscious is lunatic."

She gave me a pat on the back, "Uh-oh. You might want to leave this place for a second. Tell Carly to go to the restroom with you. Just say you can't find the place. You'll know why later. Now go."

I nodded, it was just like the old times when Claudia gets all bossy on me. Guess she never changed even if she's up there with the guy upstairs. Carly was grabbed by me when she demurred at first but realized I was pulling her around.

"Alright, alright. I'll lead you to the place. What's the hurry? We are going to be here for another hour. I saw you gazing at the ferris wheel. Are you okay?"

"Yeah, I'm fine." I paused, "It's just…"

"What is it?"

"Claudia."

"Your sister?" She frowned.

"I…" I gazed at her, "Saw her. Is it even

pragmatical for me to see her? What if she's omnipotent and wants to punish me for my ignominious sin?"

"Okay…I thought we went through this. It's only an illusion and you have to unfetter your memories about Dylan and Claudia." She stared at my blank face, "Alright then…you actually saw her? What was it like? What about Dylan? Was he there too?"

"No…" I scrutinized her face, she wasn't serious,"Haha, very funny. You must think that I'm crazy. You will never understand it." I walked away.

"Wait." She caught up to me while I was heading towards the school bus, "I do understand."

"Oh, of course you do, Ms. richest-man's-daughter." I sneered, "'Oh, daddy look, my Givenchy purse was not dry-cleaned. I'm going to throw it away. Can you buy me another one?'"

Carly sighed, "Look, when my nana died three years ago, I was devastated, She was the only one who was close to me in my family. I'm unlike you, Aurora." She looked at my exasperated face and waited for my response.

"I can't believe you are calling me by my middle name on our school bus." I murmured, told her to sit down beside me and buckle up.

She laughed, "I thought you saw the middle name coming since you were being livid at me a second ago. But I sometimes wonder how we became friends. We are so…different. At least Cheryl treats you well, and so did Dylan and Claudia. For me, it was like living in a gothic fairytale.

Everyone abhorred me, including my mother. The others in the family said I'm the devil's child because they were expecting a boy as they heard from the doctor. They hated me only because I was a girl. It was the utmost abasement."

"So…basically they are all sexist pigs."

"Something like that." She looked away, "My family had everything planned out for this unborn boy before I was born. Family heritage, the industry, everything. If I was a boy, I'd be golden. Instead, I'm just some pathetic mean girl who does not live up to their expectations. And nana was like a harbinger… always warning me about their confidential machinations."

"How do you end up here then?"

"Easy." She shrugged like it was no big deal, "My family said boarding school is for the alcoholics and the drug addicts. I guess I'm both to them and they incarcerated me. What about you? Any other reasons besides you only having Cheryl?"

"Not in particular." I raised my eyebrows, "Cheryl wanted the best for me, you know. Besides, we have Mercedes as school buses and great food. And of course, the headquarters. The people there are all pragmatists and are all super opulent."

Carly nodded.

There were about 20 people on this bus. Most of the kids were from varsity swimming, couple of them are from the jv team, there were athletes from other teams too, and there were also the coach and the driver.

"Hey what happened there?" Carly looked towards the two kids sitting at the very back of the bus. Harper Stewart was sobbing and screaming.

"Hey Stewart, are you okay?" I asked. She was covered in bruises and cuts. Blood — covered her ankles, she was sanguinary. Poor girl. Carly and I took Geometry with her and her boyfriend, Jason Roberts. And… Jason's Carly's ex. They broke up 'cause Carly was drunk and she went cruising with jocks on Jason's birthday party. Heard a lot about him last year. I often questioned Carly where her dignity was when we talked about the accident and when she's jealous about Jason and Harper. Overall, they make a fine couple.

"Her purse fell off of her seat. She attempted to pick it up but the ferris wheel already took off, so she flew off of her seat and landed on the ground. I took her to the school nurse that had her troop in the amusement park for temporary emergency recovery. The nurse said her spinal cord was severely injured, which led to temporary paralysis. I wanted to take her to the hospital, but she insisted to be here on the bus and she said she will take care of herself once she got back to school. Hang in there, Harper. You are going to be okay, we are most there." Said Jason sitting beside the seat next to Harper.

"Are you crazy?" I raised my voice and asked him, "Can't you see the blood, are you blind? You have to get her to the hospital." Harper was screaming and her legs were practically paralyzed. I would've known, I had a similar experience. A lot less blood though.

"Mr. Smith, Mr.Smith." Jason yelled at the bus driver, "Can you get us to the nearest hospital as quick as possible? Please you have to help Harper. She can't suffer this any longer."

The driver stared at him through the rear view mirror, and then he turned around to look at me and Harper. He nodded.

"What were you thinking?" I yelled at Jason, "You can't let someone who tripped and fell bleed on a bus like this…"

"She insisted." He said placidly, "She threatened to break her own feet if I don't carry her onto the bus."

"It doesn't matter!" I shouted, "You get them to a freaking hospital if there is blood everywhere! At least call an ambulance, jeez."

Jason signed. All the people on the bus were staring at me in silence. I deplored my volume when Carly looked worried.

"Are you okay?" Carly asked.

I looked back at her and nodded.

The bus stopped. A black and red pentagon appeared at the front. The Concord County Hospital.

"As you requested." Said the driver, "I'm not a monster. Get the girl to the hospital now. Chop chop!"

I thanked him. Jason carried Harper down from the school bus and headed to the hospital. The rest of the people on the bus followed. It was not a sagacious idea with that many people, but they were all in the state of trepidation ever since the school took the blame on them for Madison's suicide.

"Anyone? Doctor? Please help, my girlfriend is dying." Jason sounded so callow.

A crowd surged upon us. Harper was put on a bed by the doctors. Jason was terrified and Carly tried to calm him down, but there was no use. The scene was chaotic.

"You can't go inside." Said the doctor to Jason, "Family only. We will call her parents. You should wait with the others at the lobby."

Jason walked towards the rest of us and sat at the open seat next to Carly.

"I don't know what I'm going to do without her." Jason murmured quietly. He was in tears. Carly quickly comforted him by putting her arms around him.

20 minutes later, Harper's parents came in a hurry. Ms.Stewart kept on blaming Jason for letting her daughter go on the ferris wheel with him.

"It should've been you who's in that bed right now." She complained loudly, "Why wouldn't you grab her wallet for her?"

"She kept on telling me she got it…I never thought…"

"Well, by now you should know every time when she said she got something, she never got it. I never liked you anyway."

"I can't watch this." Said Mr.Stewart besides his wife, "Calm down now, Ellen. Have a seat." He said while wrapping a blanket around her shoulder.

Ms.Stewart, of course, pushed him away and gave him a loud, "Don't tell me to calm down" before she went off hastily and shut the door behind her.

Carly, Jason and I waited there for the entire night along with Harper's cranky mom, whom came back from the thrift shop beside the hospital at last and the incompetent dad who has no clue about how to deal with his wife for the whole night.

In the morning, all of us were awakened by a despairing scream. Several doctors rushed to the room that Harper was in. After a while, the doctor told us we could visit and perhaps say goodbye.

"Harper was strongly affected by her jitters. The accident did not treat her well. Frankly, her current situation was execrable. We have done our best but currently she's in shock. We are uncertain about the future. I'm here to represent the hospital to show our apologies and we grieve for such wonderful child."

"Perhaps you should try harder." Ms.Stewart deprecated them, she sobbed quietly. Mr.Stewart held her.

We went to Harper's room. The girl was wearing a paper-thin hospital gown and  lying on her bed still. De ja vu. It was just like the times when mother was sick. Perhaps I should never do what I had done with Dylan and Claudia. In that case, I should probably in exchange for a mother or a father. Watching Harper lying there was like checking upon the angel of death who came to Concord. Jason held her hand and pled for her to wake up. Carly's eyes were longing for him for the whole time while he was doing that.

"Of course he's going to pull a Romeo and Juliet." Said Carly, trying to cheer me up, "He looks like a pathetic hobo."

I laughed, "You don't know that for sure, jeez. Are you sure you understand what a hobo is? 'Cause I'm sure you are ambiguous about the meaning."

She nudged me for deriding her.

"Visiting hours are up." Said the nurse who appeared at the door, "Come back tomorrow."

The three of us left the hospital. The swimming coach arranged us a taxi to take us back to school. There were only once or twice when Carly asked the driver trivial details. As for the rest of our way to come back to school, everything was trite and all we had was awkward silence.

Carly went to talk to Jason when we got back. And as soon as I sat on my own bed back at my double without Carly, my phone rang, I answered cantankerously.

"Hi, Alexia Lively here."

"Hello Alexia."

Harper's voice.

"Harper?" I asked the voice inside my phone.

"Yes, it's me." Said the voice coldly. I can barely recognize the enthusiastic girl who says hi to me every time I passed the hall.

"You woke up? That's great news! I should tell…"

"Don't you dare tell anyone about this

phone call, you hear me? I'm calling you from heaven."

"I thought you were in shock."

"Oh, I'm way more than that." The voice sneered lukewarmly, "I think I've been purified. I'm reincarnated from a fire. I had an amelioration. Like I'm a phoenix, reborn, you know. God finally saw my potential as an impoverished girl. Now everything feels great."

"So where are you now? Are you in the hospital?"

"I'm in heaven, I told you."

"What do you want me to do? Are you still human?"

"One, tell no one about this phone call, we will keep in touch." She desisted, "And two, I'm surprised, Lively. Regarding the question about my form…

I'm already dead."

# FOUR



**SOME PEOPLE SAY I LIVE IN A DREAM THAT I COULD NEVER BE ABLE TO WAKE UP FROM.**

I cannot disagree.

Yet I cannot eliminate people's carping.

"On behalf of the presence of Harper's family who declined to be with us today. The Concord penguins will not ever be the same again…" said Principle Walter standing in the center of the gym. He seemed to be drowned in the tumult since he was a lummox.

"You know," Carly started, "Jason will probably move somewhere that he won't be able to be referred as 'the dead girl's boyfriend.'"

"Aw..you will miss him?"

"Of course." She sighed.

"I certainly do remember sophomore year when someone told me 'oh my gosh, my ex boyfriend is a scumbag.' I thought he turned your mental state from amiable to despondent." I smirked at her.

"Well, he changed for the better. Harper changed him." She smiled inadvertently, "I will miss her a lot."

Principal Walter welcomed Jason onto the podium, "I met Harper on the second term of sophomore year. She was one of the Concord Penguins. Diligent and pure. Innocent and wholesome. She was one of the best people that I've ever encountered. As for her death, it was my responsibility and my fault. It was all my fault..." said Jason standing at the center of the gym.

"Let's go, Roberts! Don't be such a sissy." Said one of the tyro on the baseball team at the audience.

"I should've stopped her when she reached for the purse. And I did not stop her...that's enough sadness for today. Let's focus on the better, Harper Stewart had brought joy and light into the hearts of each and every one of us. I will forever be grateful for the existence of Harper and a part of me will always, always, always save for Harper Stewart. Thank you."

The crowd applauded.

"Aw..that was lovely coming from little JR." Harper's voice castigated, "He should miss me. I was the perfect one for him. It is what it is."

"Carly," I grabbed my best friend sitting besides me, "Did you hear what she said?"

"Hear what?" Asked Carly, "I heard nothing besides Jason and his awful speech."

"The overt voice..."

"What voice?' Carly and Harper's voice occurred simultaneously, Harper scorned, Carly continued, "Are you okay, recently? You are acting all weird."

"Forget I've ever mentioned it."

"Alright then. Let me know if you need anything, 'cause I'm pretty sure I can get you some aspirin from the school nurse." Said Carly sanguinely, "I'm apprehensive that something might be flagrant and inexpedient."

I nodded, learning that she would never understand the situation that I'm currently in, "Thanks for the support."

"No problem, princess." She chuckled.

"Stop. I told you to never call me that."

She laughed and stared at Jason who came back from the center of the gym to the audience, "At least you will be able to see Cheryl today after a week of lachrymose tragedies. I'm sure she could come up with an explanation with those lunatic voices that's happening inside your head."

"Hey, I'm not crazy." I nudged her.

"Whatever you say, princess." She said caustically and raised her eyebrows while she watched me shaking my head in front of her.

Carly always calls me a 'princess' whenever she thinks I'm overreacting. Something about 'Princess Aurora' was the most fitted term for me when I'm being histrionic and bossy. And of course, any excuse to call me by my middle name was incipient. Cheryl said Dylan and Claudia came up with it the day she "adopted" us. However, Dylan said mom is the one who loved the name. I guess he abrogated it because he was too embarrassed to admit the truth.

"That's the end of our weekly assembly. Please evacuate the place orderly and safely, or else I'm going to pull the fire alarm." Said the principal while watching the freshmen wriggle around in the gym without lining up.

As I followed Carly to leave the gym, I couldn't help but wonder if Cheryl would call my name and show off her Ferrari when she picks me up today. I have my own presentiment, but how am I suppose to handle the "wealthy jinx" rumor when I'm back on Monday? I wish she would chill out and circumvent her lame comebacks with the moms.

"Hey, I'm gonna go now, my dad lets me drive today." Said Carly, waving.

I waved back and watched her find her family Volvo with her dad sitting in it in the parking lot at the back of the lawn towards where I'm headed.  The pickup spot was right besides the lawn. As I watched every one of the kids  in my grade leave, although a couple of them were still there, I never spot a vague figure of the red head nor does a tremendously loud voice appeared to  call my name.

"Cheryl had gone to the devil…" Harper's voice emerged again, she sounded like it was unequivocal, "She would never come back even if you prayed for it."

"Keep your mouth shut, you haunting psycho!" I shouted with animosity while threw the boulder that I picked up in the fountain on the lawn.

Jason and the others who were there stared at me curiously like I'm some schizophrenic patient who just came out of the hospital who never recovered. I rolled my eyes after I heard their censorious comments.

"Are you okay?" Asked Jason, staring. His face was paler than usual. I hate it.

"I'm fine." I shrugged, "The voice inside me is just so annoying."

"Wait..you hear it too? Harper's voice?" He examined my face carefully, I felt more incongruous than usual, "It started after the doctor told us the news, right? It's like a malediction."

"Oh my gosh, yes. You heard it, right? Yet Carly thinks I'm becoming wackier everyday."

He laughed, "Harper sounds so..different. I know you can talk to her through the voice, but I can't. I have seen you do it before, so I can only hear her. I cannot believe her for talking to you like that. She became so..inhuman."

"I know. Never got to know the apathetic side of her." I said while shaking my head nonchalantly.

"Hey, I did not see Mrs.Lively here today." A red BMW stopped in front of us, "I can let my driver drop you off if you want."

"I'd love that, thank you." I followed him into the car while wondering what happened to punctual Cheryl today.

"So why isn't Mrs.Lively here? She used to be on-time every single day." Asked Jason curiously, "And she looked so young…"

I chuckled, "She's not my mother to start off. She's…let's just say my foster family's sister who gets paid for taking care of me and sending me to boarding school. She's only about 22."

"That explains. I'm sorry about your family. Now I remembered Carly told me your mom died of cancer and you father died of a car accident. Let me know if you wanna talk, I'm always here for you." He was not diffident when he said that.

Huh, player. I thought to myself, I guess that's why Carly fell for him but "Thanks." Was all I came up with to say to him. I got off from the red vehicle and said goodbye as quickly as I can. I found the backup key under the plant and burst through my house's door.

"Cheryl!" I yelled, "Cheryl, I'm home!"

I scrutinized the first floor of the house. I guess it was variegated. It was still the Tiffany blue kitchen. The exact transparent fruit bowl was filled with apples on the squared white table in front of the blue stove. The counters above the stove were unscathed and filled with silver tableware, ceramic bowls, a variety of spice bottles and cereal boxes. An entire set of white sofa was still perfectly untouched and seemed like Cheryl had puffed those red squared medium-sized pillows yesterday. She had her proclivity towards crimson and she still hasn't changed the gothic wallpaper for the entire house. I remembered her being fanatical with anything that was dark red. Blood, in particular. Claudia told me that Cheryl's first boyfriend was an indifferent charlatan and took a blood oath with

her when they were ready to engage or
something. It still appalls me today. With a blue
and blackish spiral staircase behind the sofa set, it
reached us to the second floor.

The rooms of mine and Cheryl's were
separated with an extravagant restroom in
between. The door of my room was on the left
and Cheryl's was on the right.

"Cheryl? Where are you? Come out please,
I'm not in the mood for this! I just been through a
week of living in Hades' dungeon, and I'm not going
back there!"

Silence. Nothing and no one was
moving. Something was off. I opened my plain
white door but Cheryl was not there. The green
wallpaper on the wall and a tiny fireplace under
the bookshelf was the same as I left it there a
week ago. My bed was at the left corner.
Perhaps a paragon for contrast. Black sheets,
black pillow and white blankets. A blue dresser
was placed beside my purple table and chair at
the right, and a medium-sized white closet that
was enough to put all my wardrobe in. Still,
Cheryl was still not in there.

I rushed out to the hall and knocked on
Cheryl's door. She added a colossal but signature
"I.O" on her white door in red. No one respond. I
entered her room.

A queen-sized bed for her to sleep in in
gray. A dresser next to it occupied most of the
space along with her entire makeup set on the
table. I could imagine her using her brush and
play the pussycat dolls before she left to work for

the headquarters. Looking back beside the door was a malleable red  beanbag lying in front of her pink closet. Classic Cheryl.

I headed to her black and white table and chair at the right, the set was gigantic and off proportional compares to rest of the furniture in the room. And  that was where her paperworks were located since she had her fanaticism  about the headquarters. Great, at least she left a note.

*"Hey  Claudia,*

*If you are checking this note, it means something terrible had happened and I will have to deal with it. Don't upbraid me.*

*I've encountered a mysterious and confidential mission provided by the headquarters. They want to do it antediluvian style. It would be a dilemma for me if I tell you the name of the man and Cheryl would definitely chastises me for that, 'cause what I aim for tonight is surprisingly omnipotent, not going to cower though.*

*If I haven't come back in 72 hours, go to the police and file a missing person report fastidiously. Give Cheryl this letter and tell her to hold on to it for a while. If fortunate, Aurora will never see this during her lifetime.*

*All the best,*

*DL"*

"Dylan?" I asked the prodigious room, "I knew he liked my middle name. But where's Cheryl? Please tell me she's just on a simple mission which involves no-life risking."

I headed to the other spiral staircase at the end of the second floor. The third floor was a loft. We used it to place my family's legacy. And the materials that Cheryl needed when she first joined the headquarters. Oh, and of course, with our sufficient space of our loft, a medium-sized carousel was placed there, and it was not some serendipity. Dylan, Claudia and I used to be on it all the time when we first start to live with Cheryl. I guess she wanted to kept it as a memory.

I found the contact book for I.O from last year. I certainly do hope that most of the staff were still there and not killed by those parasites who went against us.

Cheryl used to call the headquarters "an upgraded version of regular child protection service". Dylan, Claudia and I were trained for self-defense mostly. The headquarter's activities were mainly underground and mostly undercover. Often times we target the cult that got infuriated by one or another. The rest of the headquarter call them the Elysium. Some say that they worship the ancient devil in Italy. Their religion was sacrosanct, and the paramount law for them was to go after "sinners" — there are no innocent mistakes. No one found out X's background, but we deemed that he's with the Elysiums.

"Dr. John?" The receiver at the headquarters picked up, "Did Cheryl check in today?"

"No. She's on a personal holiday. Why? Did something happen?" Dr. John asked quickly.

"No, no, not at all." I lied, "I'm sure she just went grocery shopping."

Personal holidays were ones where the staff at the headquarters went on a confidential mission. For the ones who have a foster family to take care of, they would usually leave a note or take their foster family kids to do the mission together. Although once the kids reached 18, the headquarters will assign those to them, they could choose and select one assignment from the scale of 1 to 10. That's how most of the people got killed. That's how Claudia and Dylan died.

"Did she leave you a note?" "Yes, but not written by her." "Not her but who?"

I sighed, "You wouldn't want to know."

"Have a nice day, ma'am."

He hung up.

I heard engines noises downstairs, "Lively, are you in there?" "Hold on, I'm coming."

I rushed downstairs and opened the door. I spot a blurred view of a blonde. Outside, the man was wearing a pair of sunglasses, the signature "I.O" shirt, a coal black leather jacket, a pair of black jeans and the classic Converse. The classic I.O uniform set. His coal black motorcycle provided by the headquarters was laying outside of my door.

"Dr. John?" I asked the man, "Come on in?"

I never officially met Dr.John in the past, but I do recognize the typical features of the British, especially with the blatant manner of his short scar on the left cheek of his face. Dr. John was in his mid-20s. Rumors had it that he buried one of the Elysium alive, when we were only supposed to capture the assassins from the opponent who went against us. The headquarters would train them to become one of ours. That's how Dr. John ended up being the receiver. At least, according to what I've heard.

"I have unfortunate news." He waited for my response, I simply stared, he continued, "I don't know how to break this to you…"

"Just do it."

He gazed into my eyes and everything else stopped.

"Cheryl went missing."

# FIVE

**IT'S A MONTH BEFORE NEW YEAR.**

And I'm in an advanced state of inebriation.

Everything was vapid. Piece by piece, crashing and kindled in front of me in slow motion while dusts flew around in the air and went straight  into my eyes. Pain took over me, I couldn't feel a thing. I guess I'm a masochist and always an individualist.

Carly and I devoted ourselves to SAT practices after the Thanksgiving holiday for the last week of November. I received the news from Dr. John when Thanksgiving holiday first started.

Dr. John recommended me to see the therapist at the headquarters. He spent Thanksgiving with me and brought me a turkey, the atmosphere became felicitous with his presence and that appeased me. The entire house would be vacuous if he wasn't here. Dr. John laughed when I told him I thought he was 25 and said he was only 19, "You also thought I was a murderer."

I stared, and he continued, "We were all recruited by the headquarters at relatively a young age. The more experienced would train the fledglings. Headquarter invitations were sent out by Dr. Marco and his wife, Dr. Kelly, aka my brutal parents. Others might bring potential candidates to seek their  approvals. Like your family. That's how we get foster families and expand our human resources." He said after he contacted the headquarters to let them approve his staying at my house for the entire holiday while he slept on the sofa in the living room. He usually isn't up until noon, and his mood gets fickle every time I called him a sluggard, but he inferred that he was a soothsayer of mood. I quitted arguing with him.

"It's better than answering phone calls everyday. Dr. Olive would take my place. Besides, I haven't gotten out of that place for 11 months. Might as well get some fresh air. And no, I did not bury an Elysium alive, only because my parents want to punish me for not taking over their family business. I.O took a lifetime for my father to do his businesses." He examined my face while I stared at him blankly, "Hey school starts today, should I drop you off?"

"No, thanks." I rejected him quickly.

"So, what? The Roberts boy can give you a ride and I can't?" He smirked while seeing me frown, "What? I have surveillance cameras to your surroundings. It was fun watching you from the headquarters. How do you think I get here this fast?" He sounded so juvenile.

I derided him for stalking me and finally

agreed to let him drop me off at school.

"You know, I'm only 2 years older than you, right?" He asked me in a circumspect tone on our way to school on his greased motorcycle, "Stop calling me Dr. John. You made me look like Justin Bieber after he got married."

I bursted into laughter, "What do you expect me to call you, Mr. the headquarter's-boss-is-my-dad, sir?"

"The name is actually Caden Evans. My parents made it John to be less conspicuous to the rest of the headquarters. And of course, to go with the rumor that those parochial people brought when they created in order to prevent me from denigrating the family name." I nodded and noticed I arrived. I hopped off from his motorcycle. He followed.

"Thanks for the ride. Good luck heading back." I said to him and waved.

He raised his eyebrows and sneered, "Oh, I forgot to tell you. My dad told me to stay at yours for the another month. It isn't my fault that they don't want to take me back. Plus, they enrolled me at St.Clarke's. And you, my friend, are a day student as long as I'm here." He put one hand into his jeans' pocket, hooked his leather jacket with his index finger after he flaunted it in front of me, slung it over one shoulder, and waved while strolling towards the main building through the lawn. Leaving me with my mouth wide open in front of my dorm room.

"Alexia!" Carly's voice snapped me out of the shock, Caden was already gone, "How can you not tell me that you moved out of the dorm? I was so puzzled when Lana told me to move to a single. Did you forget about me for some boy? You know, it'd be nice to use a utilitarian device named phone and call me back?"

"I'm sorry…" I apologized, "Everything is a mess right now…"

"Alright, alright I forgive you." She rubbed my head, "Have you heard? A new kid came today, his name is John Evans."

"It's just Caden." I said to her, trying to show apathy as much as possible, "You guys already knew?"

"Of course." She scrutinized me with disapprobation, "I thought you hated the gossip. Have you met him yet? Is he.."

"Actually…" I interrupted her.

She suggested me to go on with fervor, I sighed.

"He's living with me." I was mortified after seeing Carly with her eyes wide open like a goldfish. I guess I could abandon my circuitous talk about how it was an accident..

"For a week?"

"No…For another month."

"Another?"

"He stayed with me on Thanksgiving…"

"How do you two know each other?"

I stayed silent, "Just think, and you will know."

"Alright, you should talk to me. Now, we better head to class. I have Biology, and you have French. Let's go."

We walked into the main building of

St.Clarke's. The school's mascot had been vandalized. The Concord Penguin was there without its head. Each and everyone of us was talking until Principal Walter showed up and dismissed all of us. Carly and I headed to the opposite direction.

"Can I talk to you, Ms. Lively?" Principal Walter stopped me, and I nodded. I don't have any other choice besides following him.

"Remember when I put you in charge for organizing the Christmas Vespers?" He pushed the flyers that I made at the beginning of the term, "Now, you are a bad influence to the student body, Ms. Lively…."

"How so?"

"I can't let a missing guardian's kid work for my school events, you know that."

"But—"

"No, buts, Ms. Lively. You know the deal." He coughed to disguise his embarrassment, "Oh, and your cousin, Mr. Evans isn't it? I heard he's staying at your house. You should go ahead and take care of him while the county police try and find your sister, shall we? I apologize and show great condolence for your loss, Ms. Lively. But you understand, right? You are free to go now."

"He's not my cousin…" The principal raised his eyebrows. I nodded quietly without saying another word.

"I'll put one of the guys on the baseball team in charge. They have strength, and I'm sure they could take care of it."

I scorned and walked out of the principal's

office. Ms. Martin already received the principal's note and gestured me to sit down. She handed back the quiz that we did last Monday, and I only received a 8/10. How can I focus on school when there's so much happening around me? Perhaps I should just ditch with Caden.

I loved Christmas Vespers. It was the only time that I felt not alone. With everyone else in the school to celebrate me. Whatever has been said and done was done with the principal. I can't fight back anymore.

Everyone was staring at me when I went to the hall. Carly hurried back by my side.

"I'm sorry, Alexia. About the Christmas Vespers."

"So you heard, huh?"

"Yeah…" She paused, "I met Caden. He's in my Biology class. Why haven't you mention that he's totally hot?"

"I—"

"Okay, I know it is a weird thing to admit your cousin is hot. But why wouldn't you warn me beforehand? Especially since you've been living with him for more than a week now. Chloe said she saw him dropping you off for school today. And why would you leave out that detail?"

"I—-"

"Is that why you did not call or text me for the entire Thanksgiving holiday? My parents were expecting you. I'm so disappointed. You do realize you can FaceTime me right? It's not that hard, Alexia."

"For the second time, he is not my

cousin and he just showed up."

"You expect me to believe that."

"Yes, Carly. Why would I lie to you?" I shrugged, "It isn't my fault that you won't believe me."

"Okay, now you even sound like Caden." She signed, "Fine…tell me what happened."

"He showed up after…"

"Hey Alexia." Jason interrupted me, "Did Mrs. Lively give you a ride today? Tell her I said hello."

Carly stared at Jason, "It's not Mrs. Lively! Actually, never mind. Why wouldn't Cheryl give Alexia a ride?"

Jason stared back at her, "I heard she went missing. I think that's wild. Isn't that right, Alexia?"

Both of them waited for my response while I scratched my head.

"Cheryl is still missing." A voice behind me appeared, "Why do you think I've been living at hers? And not just because I'm her distant relative."

"You are not my distant cousin, Caden!" I yelled at Caden behind me while seeing him stood beside and smirked at Jason, "Stop telling everybody that. It's gonna be really weird if I'm living with you, isn't it?"

He gave Jason a high five, "How you doing, Roberts?"

"Ugh!" I rolled my eyes and pulled Carly from standing between the two disrupting boys and left them behind.

"Hey!" She yelled at me, "I was actually

enjoying that!"

"Shut up." I nudged her, "Do you want me to explain what happened or not?"

"Okay, okay. Do your thing." She said while putting her hand up.

"So before the Thanksgiving holiday started, Friday, Cheryl did not show up to pick me up. You always knew she was punctual. I waited after seeing all the kids at the spot leaving, but she was not there. I noticed something wrong, but I could not find out why. You know how the foster family system works in the headquarters, right? She did not even leave me a note. Instead, she left a note that Dylan wrote…"

She stared, "Your brother? In your brother's handwriting?"

"Yes…it was a note that he left for Claudia…right before he went on the  X mission. He also mentioned if lucky, I would never have to see that note in my life. I guess something tragic actually happened. I mean, what would I do without Cheryl? What am I suppose to do without her in my life? I can't live without her…she's like my surrogate mother or something. "

She put her arms around me, "It's okay, it's okay. I'm sure they would find her. There's no way that Cheryl would leave you. She cares about you too much to do that…" She said while entered the library with me.

"But what if she's just…gone? Like Madison and Harper? What if… what if I made her do whatever she did to herself?" I sat down and gestured her to grab a seat.

"No, no. It was not your fault that Madison and Harper were gone. It's not like Harper or Madison's ghosts were haunting you." She said cheerfully.

I stared, "I haven't been quite honest with you recently. Our dorm room.. before we switched to the double that we are in, was a crime scene. Madison wrote me 'it was all our fault.'"

"I'm aware." She paused, "Anything else?"

"That voice I've been constantly asking you about…it was Harper's voice. She..called me after we left the hospital and said she's in heaven being reincarnated. She kept on mocking me. I thought you might hear it too but you could not. Turns out it was Jason who could hear her and that's why I accepted his ride on Friday."

She showed interests, "Makes sense, continue."

"After I came back home, I looked everywhere and I cannot find her. Honestly, she didn't even say anything. I tried to call the headquarters since personal devices weren't allowed to use I.O.. Dr. John…Caden picked it up and he came to tell me that Cheryl went missing. I couldn't find a way to tell you, I don't know what you will think of me or expect you to believe me. I was too messed up to call or text you on Thanksgiving and I can't be a burden to you or Mr and Mrs. Cooper. They treated me so well and I just can't let them down." I stared into Carly's green eyes and looked away.

She kept on scrutinizing me and I know she's

judging. At least, I told her what was happening, that'd be a relief.

She bursted into laughter while the librarian tried to shush her, but it was no use. Everyone else stared in her direction, and she finally poised herself after two or three minutes.

"Jesus, thank god." She tittered and said, "Now I know you are actually a weird sociopath."

I frowned while watching her laugh all over the place.

"Those were obviously the mendacious reasons! How dare you make up such nonsense to fool me? You thought I was some ingenue kid?" She disparaged me, "Just admit you are dating your cousin and don't want to spend Thanksgiving with me and my family, I would've understood. Don't be such an ingrate! You're constantly lying to my face and it's not just some peccadillo that I can overlook and it's not venial. I swear, Alexia, if I kept being friends with you,  I would become a fly-by-night just like you." She was in a flustered manner and walked out of the library.

The rest of the day was pretty much the same. Besides people coming up to me to congratulate me for having a distant cousin. I quitted explaining to them that Caden's not my cousin of any sort by lunchtime. I went back to my dorm as usual but I felt a grip behind me and dragged me out of the building.

"Carly?"

"Let's go."

Without any warnings, I was already in front

of the motorcycle.

"I will see you at practice tomorrow?" Jason said to Caden while he threw the hockey stick at him.

Caden waved at him and told me to sit. Loads of people overcrowded the parking lot to see Caden, he started the engine and we were ready to go.

"So…" I broke the silence, "Varsity hockey? On your first day?"

"Catfight with Carly?"

"How did you…"

"Since when did you start to care about me? I'm not even your distant cousin."

"I didn't mean to…"

"It's not your fault." He replied quickly, "You need to have something to clear the rumor about how I'm staying at yours, right?"

"Right…" I nodded, "I apologize for yelling."

"That's okay. But you got to trust me from now on."

"I'll try." I stared into his sparkling eyes, "Thanks for everything."

"Of course." He glanced back at me covertly, "Maybe you can make it up to me."

"Ain't no way."

"Darn it." He shrugged, "Worth a shot."

I tittered stilly while he petted on the head. Somehow I saw through his tenderness. The way he put up a charade so effortlessly in front of others as if his bitterness was purposeless. Or is this another one of his gimmicks? I could not tell, but he was all I have now.

We arrived at my house. Caden stepped in front of me before we went in.

"Now before we go in," He gazed at me, "go sit on the sofa."

"Why?"

"Just trust me."

I obeyed him, he went in and stood in front of the fireplace on the monotoned carpet.

"I have…disappointing news." He stared into my eyes with veracity, "Cheryl is dead."

"NO!" I shouted desperately, "NO! NO! NO! NO!" "I'm sorry but…"

"Did you get this from the headquarters? There must been some kind of mistake. There is no way that Cheryl is dead! What does it say on the autopsy report? Where's the body?"

He stayed silent for a minute, "She left you and I'm sorry."

"How could she do this to me? I don't get it!" I sounded so puerile. With Carly's specious accuses and Cheryl's disappearing act, I had no one. At least… my "distant cousin" could help.

"Do you want me to get you low fat ice-cream?" He asked, "I heard you people like that stuff."

"What's wrong with you? This isn't a breakup.." I yelled at him fractiously while seeing him raised his left eyebrow, "On second thought, that'd be a good idea. The real one not the crappy kind from Walmart."

He grabbed a bucket of ice-cream from the refrigerator and two giant spoons, "I know it's winter but it might assuage you." He smiled and popped open the bucket. I dug a semi-circular size of the ice-cream in the bucket and shoved it into my mouth; it was cold but sweet.

Outside, snowflakes started to fall from the sky. A bucket of strawberry ice-cream and I was cuddling with Caden on the sofa in front of the fireplace.

"I'm gonna miss you when you're gone." I said to him while saw him cogitated.

"Will you forget me?"

"Why would I?"

"Hey," He put his arms around me, "I won't leave you. And when you wake up next morning, I will be right by your side. It's late, go to sleep."

He put the ice-cream bucket down, collected the spoons and carried me to my room upstairs. He put a blanket over my shoulder after he put me on my bed. I stayed stagnant.

"Good night, Alexia."

"Night, cousin." I watched him turned off the lights and walked out of the room. I fell asleep quickly.

[...]

I woke up the next morning.

"Shoot, I'm late." I checked my alarm and found it says 11:30am. I quickly put on my uniform and headed downstairs, "Caden? Caden, why won't you wake me up! Are we still going to school together?"

I found he was not there. The red-square pillows on the sofa was placed exactly the way it did before Thanksgiving. I peeked out of the window, the motorcycle was gone.

"Stupid fraud! I'm such an idiot."

I pulled out my phone and tried to call the headquarters but no one picked up. I jogged to school straight to the ice skating rink but no one was there. I hurried down and knocked on Carly's dorm room, but no one responded. Not even Lana was there.

Carly was still giving me cold eyes and ignored all of my texts and calls. She even changed her voicemail to "If your last name's Lively, quit calling me". And without Caden, everything was crashing down.

I sprinted back home.

First floor…

the medicine cabinet…

the second shelf…

not this one…not that one…that's not it…ibuprofen…Benadryl…Xanax…Xanax!

There we go.

One, two, three, four, five, six, seven. Good enough.

Water…chug it down…chug it down…

Death…Madison, Harper, Cheryl…all dead.

Something was tearing my heart out, a beast trampled on my heart, shot a poisoned arrow, and pierced the center of my heart.

Mom, Dad, Claudia, Dylan…dead. All dead because of me.

Chug it down… chug it down…

Everything will be over soon.

My view became obfuscated. For a moment, I was insentient.

And then…everything went black.

# PART B

# SIX

**I MUST BE IN HEAVEN.**

…Until I found out I was facing the ceiling with a nurse by my side.

"Hey, you woke up." Said the nurse, staring, "How do you feel? You must have a new malady, and I reported it back to the headquarters to let them figure it out."

"Cheryl?" I frowned, "What are you doing here? I must be in heaven. Or else why are you here? I thought you left me."

"That's absurd. I would never leave you." She censured me but smiling.

"Then what happened to Caden?"
She tittered, "Dr. John?"

I nodded with blankness, "Did he leave me like you did? Why am I still alive? I don't get it, what's happening to me? Am I turning into a freaking werewolf?"

Cheryl rolled her eyes, "No, yes and no. He's

right here and he'll explain everything." She pointed at the bench behind her. A figure in black appeared.

I gasped at his direction and saw him feigning sleep, "Why can't you explain the whole thing to me?"

"Dr. Coleman, please report to the emergency room for patient #1289's surgery." A speaker above me shouted.

Cheryl stood up without answering my question, "I'll leave you two to it." She stared at Caden, "You almost got me, Brandy. Duty calls." then she waved and strolled out of my room

"Caden?"

"Don't worry, I'm here." He said without opening his eyes. We stayed silent for a moment

"Why did you leave me? What is happening to me?"

"I didn't. I'll explain."

"The principal even told me you dropped out of school. What do you mean 'I didn't'?"

He sighed, "My parents wanted me to reconsider their offers and they called a family meeting saying that I should not be at yours all the time, which I don't mind, personally."

"Then why did it take so long?" I asked him innocently, "I was waiting and you didn't even wake me up!"

"Sorry about that." He scratched his head, "I enjoyed watching you sleep…"

"It's creepy."

"It's romantic." He smirked, "I was going to but you slept so peacefully…"

"Did you at least stay the night?" I asked

and gazed into his eyes.

"Yes..."

"Did we..."

"No." He said quickly, "Nothing happened."

"Are you sure you did not roofie me and..."

"If I did, you won't even know I'm there."

"So you've done it before?"

"Yeah," He laughed after seeing my face, "When I annexed one of the Elysiums."

"Oh, so you actually captured one."

"Oh yeah, I made a fine shooter until they made me the receptionist."

I looked at him, "Don't digress the topic. I thought the purpose of the  headquarters is to heal people and teach them self defense. Can you please elaborate what is happening to me?"

"That's part of it."

"What do you mean? Why am I still alive? Wait, how the heck am I alive? I thought I committed suicide...and what the heck is Cheryl doing here undercover as a surgeon?"

"Thought you did not care since the first thing that you asked was did we do it." He raised his eyebrows while I nudged him, "Okay, here's the thing. What do you think I.O stood for?"

"As in I.O for headquarters?" I gazed and he nodded, "I mean, international occupation?"

He laughed, "Wrong. Immortal

Organization."

I frowned, "What?"

"Immortals." He pronounced lucidly.

"So…vampires?"

"Haha, I wish but no." He looked into my eyes, "Honestly…not until now."

"Okay, now you are confusing me."

"No, you are. Seriously? First werewolves, now vampires? What else do you want to be? A witch? Get over your fanatical theories about Vampire Diaries, girl!"

"Hey, you don't get to judge since I'm the one who's coming back from the dead."

"Well..none of us attempted suicide before. At least, not in front of my face. Couple years ago, there was a rumor saying that X got saved when he tried to kill himself and became one of us…so in this case, it was not unprecedented and he was more of a charlatan himself, so I don't blame him."

"Okay…" I paused in diffidence, "How exactly do we become an immortal."

"It's an…Italian thing. More of a malediction."

"Italian?" I asked him, "I have no relations-"

"You might not, but your family does." He shrugged, "It's a genetic thing,  and you are one of the paradigms. In fact, you are the paragon."

"Okay…so, how old are you then?" I asked him charily.

"19."

"I meant how long."

"About 175 years."

"….when did you know that you are a… that?"

"I had my theories, and when my parents finally recruited me to I.O…"

I nodded, "How old is Cheryl then?"

"About 220.."

"Then how can I have no memories of my Italian heritage or whatever?"

"The I.O started to give us medical treatments after you got in. Those drugs could make you to revise your past memories. They might have…modified it."

"Okay…" I processed the whole thing in my mind, "Then explain to me explicitly how I became one of you?"

"You did not 'become' one of us. In fact, you are from the original family, Princess Aurora." He smirked at me, "Ring a bell?"

I shivered and frowned, it does ring a bell. De ja vu. Is that why I hated so much when people call me by my middle name?

"I don't understand." I stared at him, trying to comprehend this dilemma. "Which part?"

"Basically…" I paused, seeing him watching me with amusement, "Everything."

"I know, it's confusing. But you have to get some rest before the nurse kicks me out." He got up and left without saying another word.

"Ouch!" Something inside me was knocking on my head.

"Why what happened? Did I step on you?" Caden turned around.

"No, just go. I'll be fine." I waved at him.

He nodded and left.

"Ouch! Jesus!" The pain coming from the deep core of my head started to eschewing me from the inside out.

One hit…

an image of…a house?

Two hits…

a wooden door…

Three hits…

a doorknob…

My head was spinning in a circle like a toy train. Everything in front of me was obfuscated.

My consciousness faded as I laid on the bed while I stopped fighting the pain and the urge to be awake.

I fell asleep.

# SEVEN

**I FOUND MYSELF LOST.**

Without blinking, the identical doorknob appeared at my sight, and I twisted it.

The door cracked open without the normal squeaking sound of a wooden door. It shuttered behind me and the lights turned on.

"Hello?" I scrutinized my vicinity, "Anybody home? Hello?"

It was a prodigious house, probably owned by some wealthy but snobby family in the past. The wooden floor — seemed to be cleaned by people monthly. There were murals made out of thousands and hundreds of mosaic pieces. All of them were formed like a crossword puzzle. On the left, the picture was about  the size of a square with each side of 5 inches. It showed a relatively juvenile brunette, a girl with curly hair with a similar Audrey Hepburn face but darker eyebrows. I'd say that might be related. She was in a classic medieval red dress with black ribbons tied around her hair and a silver diamond ring on the middle finger of her left hand. She smiled gracefully at the person stood next to her while picked up a corner of her dress, ready to bow. "CKL" was handwritten in black ink at the right corner of the piece. I'm guessing those were her initials.

At the right side of the wall above a 4-legged wooden desk, the picture presented a fine image of a teenage boy. Probably just hit his puberty. He, too, had dark eyebrows and many layers of eyelashes with a surprisingly cliched looking of a modern day football player's hair… Ooh, now I know where that came from. He was in a black blazer and an old long sleeves shirt. He was staring at the person at his right side. Probably the girl on the left since the shades of the figure was mainly red.

There was a chandelier dangling from the top of the ceiling. The light dazed into my eyes and something was dripping from the top. I took two steps forward and checked. Is it water? I thought to myself. I stared at the ceiling and wondered as the water dripped on my face.

"Ah!" It dripped and my skin felt like I was burning. The poison kept on sinking and it was excruciating.

"Someone help me! Ah!" I started to scream, "Make it stop! Why is this hurting me! Get it off! Please!"

As I closed my eyes and the pain scuttled into my entire face, I woke up screaming.

"Are you okay?" Cheryl turned on the light

and rushed to me with Caden by her side.

"I'm okay, I'm okay." I said with tears in my eyes while adjusting to the light.

Caden patted my head and stared. Something's wrong.

"What is it?" I asked him and Cheryl, "Why are you two looking at me like I'm doomed when I'm actually unscathed?"

Cheryl stared at Caden and he nodded. She managed to find a small mirror from her pocket and Caden it to me. In the mirror, my hair was tangled up and wrapped around my neck. Caden unwrapped them. Conspicuous deep red marks appeared and it was like…I was strangled.

"Your hair might be choking you when you screamed…" Caden said with concerns in his eyes.

I frowned, "That's absurd. Back me up here, Cheryl." Cheryl stared, "It's true. I saw it happening. I'm sorry."

"And if that's not the worst part, look at her arms." Caden said to Cheryl while lifting up my left arm with his fingers.

Cuts and bruises. 5 cuts were shown on my left arm. Thin but deep bloody cuts like the ones you got from cutting yourself.

"Did you try and get yourself killed again?" Cheryl asked, "'Cause this is unacceptable!

"No!" I retorted quickly, "I was sleeping, you know that!"

"Now, now, Dr. Coleman, don't be so hard on her!" Caden tittered his left eyebrow and said to Cheryl, "Just tell her what happened."

"Nightmares." I frowned, "But I can't remember all the details. I just know that something toxic was dripping on my face and it caused me physical pain. I started screaming afterwards and that should be the time where the hair chocking started."

"What were you dreaming about before the poison started to kill you?" Cheryl asked, "What's the setting or the events that was happening? School? Home?"

"I can't remember." I replied quickly, "To be honest, I don't recall a thing."

"Now you have to try harder. Think, Alexia! Think!" Cheryl yelled.

My head went blank. For a moment, I can utter no words. The helpless feeling of loneliness gushed through my entire body.

"It's okay, it's okay." Caden tried to calm Cheryl down while comforting me, "She knows we are trying to help. It's late, you probably are tired…"

"What time is it?" I asked him before he started to blab.

"Four o'clock in the morning." He said concisely, "Don't be so hard on her, Dr. Coleman!"

"Kids in love these days…" Cheryl sighed, "You have to give me something, Alexia. Or else I'm just going to tell Dr. Marco and Dr. Kelly to provide me a telepathic robot to monitor your dreams. Trust me, you do not want that!"

"Ooh! Dr. Kiki and Dr. Xavier's training monkeys works! Or maybe Dr. Jeremy and Dr. Bonnie's drone can benefit you, too!" Said Caden with exultation in his eyes.

"Enough with that extraneous crap, John." Cheryl rolled her eyes when Caden scolded at her, she knew he hated the whole "Dr. John" thing since Kelly and Marco treated her better than Caden, "And don't even think that you could start jokes about vampires and werewolves. It's entirely different."

"Hey, hey, hey!" Caden showed his bristle, "She started it herself."

Cheryl shook her head and told me to have a good night before she headed out with Caden.

I tried to fall asleep but stayed wide awake.

Until the morning came with the sun and it occurred to me that I should probably head back to school.

# EIGHT

**THERE WAS LEGITIMATELY NOTHING WORSE THAN THE FRIGID WEATHER IN NEW HAMPSHIRE.**

As I followed the trace of the significant grey and blue buildings around the school's corner, I know I'll definitely gain a "death sentence".

"Bro, sick car!" Was the first thing that I heard coming from Jason, standing at the center of the lawn of the open spaced parking lot with a bunch of whole  other hockey players.

"My car, asshole!" I shouted back while dialing down my car window.

"Hey, hey, hey. I'm driving. My rules!" Caden said in the front wearing sunglasses and shut the window of my Ferrari in front of my face.

"Did I mention how terrible your driving skills are?" I said to him and watched him sneered.

"You don't want to let Cheryl drive, do you?" He started, "Besides, you can't even drive. At least I can."

"Ugh." I rolled my eyes while watched him

gloat at the driver's seat.

"You ready?" He asked.

"To do what?" I was so confused until I realized Carly was standing a mile away from the hockey players.

Her facial expression was bland as usual, but I can tell how much remorse she must have felt after not seeing me on campus for two weeks, and all of our problems were solved.

"Ah!" She screamed when she saw our car parked in front of her like she just woke up from her nightmares.

"Thank God, you are back!" She said to me after I stepped out of the car with Caden, "How's your uncle? May he rest in peace."

"What?" I stared at Carly, and looked back at Caden.

"Isn't that what happened?" Asked Carly, "Principal Walter told us that you went to visit your distant but found uncle and he died of cancer."

I tilted my eyebrows at Caden, he blinked twice to suggest we might as well go along with it, "Yeah, that's exactly what happened. Poor Uncle Mason. He was such a happy man. Life isn't fair."

Carly nodded sympathetically, "I told Lana you should move back to our double since you suffered a great loss and you should live with your best friends after coming back from Christmas break to process the whole thing. She said yes and we are roomies again!"

"Great." I said without looking at her.

With the sound of the class bell ringing,

she handed me my French textbook and nudged me towards the language building. My head went blank  again.

[…]

"Ms. Lively, please report to the principal's office." The speaker in the hall started to shout at me again.

"Really? Right before lunchtime? Are you serious? Perfect timing, Ted." I complained and frowned while headed to the principal's office.

I barged in without knocking. "Well come on in, Ms. Lively."

Principal Walter was staring at the sofa in front of him. I realized I should probably sit there.

"What do you want now, Ted? Another one of my non-distant relative died, too?"

"I know, I know." He sighed, "Before you get mad, can you please tell me why you ditched school for entire two weeks? That is inexcusable, young lady. Anyways, I begged the teachers not to fail you in every single one  of your classes. Now this is the last day of school before Christmas, at least show some spirit. You know how hard it was for me? Just answer my questions, okay?"

I stayed silent and stared at him without any awkwardness, "I can't."

He shocked his head, "I will tell you what happened, you attempted to ditch while climbing over the fence and failed. Therefore, you ended up in the  hospital. Am I correct?"

I frowned, "Who told you this?"

62

"Jason Roberts."

"Alright, sir. You are exactly right. I won't do it again. I promise."

He showed his bristle and shoved me out of his office while shaking his head and saying, "Young people these days."

"What did he say to you? Anything near the truth?" Caden appeared out of nowhere and asked like usual.

"Nope. I thought you have super hearings or something. Didn't you hear all of it?"

"I wasn't trying to pry so I wasn't paying attention."

"Okay then. Apparently Jason Roberts saw me climb over the school fence and trip, which got me sent to the hospital."

"That's insane. Did he also say he hit his head, too?"

"Shut up. There's no time for your jokes. I need to know what he saw and what happened that day."

"Better hurry up. He's sitting with Carly for lunch today. Let's go." We headed to the cafeteria; as I sat down and he shoved fro-yo in my face. Today's weird.

"You, Jason Roberts. I need to talk to you." I pointed at him while he was busy chatting with Carly, "Carly, do you mind if I steal your ex for a sec?"

"Sure thing, go ahead." Carly replied while turning her attentions to Caden. I grabbed Jason to a corner of the cafeteria, "Spill. Now. What did you tell Walter and what did you see the other day?"

"What? You fell off the fence and tripped." He chuckled.

"You know that's not true."

"Fine. My uncle worked at the hospital you were in and he overheard the nurse saying that you overdosed and tried to attempt suicide."

"You are lying."

"Why would he lie, Alexia? Don't even deny it. Explain to me how is it possible that you are alive? Could you please just fill me in?

"I can't." I said to him while stared at Caden at the distant table. He nodded, and I started, "Fine. I'm an immortal."

"What?" Jason frowned, "Please tell me this is just some kind of joke and you want to mess with me?"

"No, I'm not. You know I don't lie. Caden is, too. He will explain it to you later. Right now just put it aside."

"Okay…"

"Did you tell Carly anything?"

"Not yet. You should probably do it yourself. If you don't, then I will. Just promise me you'll tell her today…"

"Today?"

"Yes, today. She's your best friend and she deserves to know the truth. Deep down there, you know that." He paused, "And Caden's your boyfriend, not your cousin, right? I mean, at least you two have a thing."

"Fine. And no, we don't have a 'thing', Jason."

"Whatever you say."

I rolled my eyes. We went back to the table and pretended nothing was wrong, but I can't help but wonder how I should break this down to my best friend. Maybe she does deserves to know.

"Carly?" I finally started. "Yes?"

"Do you mind if I spend Christmas at your place? I mean, we haven't done it since forever and I bailed on you this Thanksgiving, so I thought I could make it up to you."

"I'd love to, oh my gosh, yes! We could totally have a slumber party right after class ends today….not sure if my parents would allow it, but it's Christmas so they should be feeling generous. At least you are welcome at my place.
What happens to Caden then?"

"I'll be fine." He said to her, "I should probably go and stay with Jason, right, dude?"

"Of course, man."

"Look at them all bromancy." Carly said to me, "Guess everything is back to normal."

"Not quite." I murmured quietly without saying another word while watching the three of them being cheerful.

[…]


"So, Alexia. We were expecting you this Thanksgiving. What happened?" Said Mrs. Cooper, riding shotgun while Mr. Cooper took the driver's seat.

"Sorry about that…I was a bit caught up with my distant cousin's business. I hope I didn't disappoint the two of you."

Carly chuckled, "Of course not, I'm just glad that you made it for Christmas, I got you a present!" She said with her usual peppy tone while rolling her eyes, "Crocodile tears…" she whispered.

"We are here."

Just like I recall from memory, the red and blue mansion appeared before my eyes. The style of the house was just as identical as the ones that were placed in this area owned by the Coopers. The Coopers Industry was once the wealthiest people in this town, always "being the top 3 of all real estate companies". Once? Oh that, it meant they were no longer the richest. Why? Because their unborn golden boy became a little girl that they never expected. Or probably because they may or may not have informed practically every single one of the bosses in business that their golden boy will inherit their family heritage, and exploit his entrepreneurial skills in the future.

Once they found out it was a girl, Mr. Cooper did everything in his power to go after the scarly-cat doctor who told them the baby was a boy. It was fortunate that Nana Cecilia was in her 50s and gave the hospital a heads-up before Mr. Cooper could do anything effective to retaliate.

On the other hand, the "vicious mom", aka Mrs. Cooper, according to Carly, sent her to an asylum when the scandal of the Coopers were spread around the country. A place named The

Elysium for Brothers and Sisters. Elysium as in the Elysium? Not exactly. You see, The Elysium of Brothers and Sisters (we go by TEBS) was originated from a Swedish family who basically adopted too many kids and the mom died, leaving the dad unemployed and having consumption in his late years. TEBS was an acronym for Tessa, Eddie, Britney and Stevie. As in the names of the original couple and the twins that they gave birth to. However, the breading process of the twins didn't happen until Tessa and Eddie were in their 40s. By then, they've already adopted 12 kids from the age range of 3 to 22. Some say Tessa and Eddie died of cancer and consumption, some say that the 22-year-old was so desperate for attention that the and the 17-year-old girl caused a gas leak to stifle most of the other kids, including the 3-month-old twins.

And of course, just as any profound institution, the 22-year-old and the 17- year-old established TEBS 240 years ago. Every time I asked Cheryl, at least trying to inquire about the reason for what made her stop by TEBS that day, she always shook her head at first, and then started to say, "war, terrible war." Just to give me a good laugh as a Hunger Games fan.

It was a good thing that a 2-year-old knows how to perform an epic jail break, so very fortunately with the size of Carly, she got out. Weirdly, Cheryl stopped by TEBS on the day and recognized her as the "insane daughter who had a mental breakdown at the age of 2 from the once wealthiest family". She contacted the headquarters and Carly got..."adopted".

So that was pretty much the story. Carly thought something has finally changed, her parents finally came to their senses and accepted her. Nana Cecilia came along with an attitude of "I rather die than stay in that hellhole".  She said to me peacefully. Carly's real parents disappeared after that day, some say that they skipped town, some say that the headquarters had taken care of them, and according most of the people, they joined the Elysium.

I know what you are thinking, regarding Carly's knowledge, no. So Nana Cecilia and I will have to put all of this in one piece and deliver it to her. Before you started to think my best friend is dumb, she was injected with this "thing"  that they gave her from the headquarters, so pretty much some of the  memories were modified.

As for the ones talking and driving previously, they were Dr. Kiki and Dr.Xavier. They were a happily married couple and of course, Carly was a bit suspicious at first, but I guess she decided she was better off this way and with the brainwash, I guess everything worked out.

# NINE

**IT WAS THE WEEK THAT I TURNED 16.**

I decided I should major in drama and minor in government. Once I get to college, I told Cheryl and Carly about it. Cheryl simply nodded and Carly teased me since all these years of being friends with her, the only thing that I can come up with is to be a drama major.

"Ouch!" I felt like I got hit in the head.

"Are you okay?"

One hit, I'm standing against the wall...

"Something's wrong." Carly panicked, "I'm going to call Cheryl."

Two hits, corridors?

"Hey Cheryl, something's——-"

"Don't!" I snatched her phone and call it quits, "I'm fine...Ouch!"

Three hits, red carpet and stairs...

"No you are as pale as a ghost! Even for you!" She shouted and tried to dial again.

Four hits, a painting...

"Alexia, can you hear me? Hello? Are you there? Stay with.." And I felt nothing.

[…]

I guess I'm in the same mansion again. Just like last time, the history repeat itself. Instead of the identical old place that I was in before, now I came a little closer. Right under where the poisoned water was dripping from last time, except this time, nothing were on the ceiling

"So…a bit further, huh?" I heard myself saying, my voice echoed.

There were still two paintings from the left to the right, both of them were  labelled AKL. The girl on the left seemed relatively young, possibly the latest new-born in the family. Like the dress that the curly hair girl wore, she was wearing a black one. With red ribbons in her black straight hair. This girl had the most exquisite facial features in the family but comparatively not that pretty compares to the other two women on the other paintings. Cherry lips, slender eyebrows, almond-shaped eyes with black eyeshadows and eyeliner that came along with a small nose. Her cheeks ceased to the usual blush like the others and she was pale while presenting a not elegant enough image. A bit clumsy, some might say and she only grinned a bit while tilting her left lip. She was looking to the left, probably staring at the figure dressed in royal blue. Her hands were free and seemed very reluctant when she used her right hand to grab the edge of her dress, it did not seemed like she bent at all but she tried to feign it anyways. A crimson heart-like necklace was on her neck, somehow I found it with high familiarity.

On the contrary, the woman on the right side of the wall was smiling with  her teeth shown. She seemed preppy and very loving. Probably the mother of her children. Unlike the girl dressed in black, she had the Audrey Hepburn eyebrows like the other two in the family. Her beauty was explained without any additional features and no one would look away. Bright red lips,  small nose and large hazel eyes, the proportion was just right and anyone would be amazed by her possible loving and kind features. She was dressed in royal blue and a corsage on her right wrist. A crown on her head with  her wary red hair featured on the side of her face. The crown was made of bronze, 12 silver diamonds on top of it, and just like any medieval crown, I assume that was definitely the queen.

Before I could observe the vicinity, I took a few steps forward. This time, very deliberately thought about the places that I should place my feet on. And  glad  to  not  get  burned  by  poison water again. The  red  carpets  and  golden  stairs were  at  the  end  of  the  corridor  was  extremely long. Well, at least it seemed like it. It was absurd how someone would use corridors and stairs as the entrance of their house, but then again, in a modern perspective, we have fireplaces in our living rooms and all they have now were strike-a-light and wood.

I took one step at a time and found the

carpets were fluffier than the other objects in the room, covered with a considerable amount of ashes and a distinct smell of smoke. Oh well, if the mosaic paintings survived, how could the carpets have gotten burned? I arrived at the second floor of the mansion without realization. There was this gigantic mosaic piece on the wall. A red wooden four-legged desk was under the painting, along with a small cubic box on the top. I wanted to open the box, but something tells me to examine the painting first.

The label was "KING VLADIMIR III". So I was right, this is the palace of a royal family. Why am I here then? The man in the painting seemed to be in his 40s. A bit of gaudy mustache below his big nose, and he did not smile. He was frowning with his slender eyebrows and his eyes were examining something as if someone just stole money from him. Oh jeez, there was no way that he was good enough for the queen. He even looked a bit like Stalin's son with that resemblance. I shook my head at the painting and felt like he looked so Bulgarian. If the painting was alive, the king must've judged me from the inside and probably would wanted to chop my head off.

However, the box on the table looked delicate. Something must be inside it, I mean, then why would they put it here? I had an impulse to put my hand on it, and as soon as I do that, a wooden stake pierced through the wall and pushed me down to the first floor. Instant pain overwhelmed me. I started to scream while watching the same old poison dripping down my throat and gradually moved up to my face.

"Help! Help! Somebody help me! Why is this happening? Carly? Carly? Carly, are you there? NO! Make it stop please, make it stop ahhhhh!"

I felt a bucket of water splashed from the top of my head. I was immediately aware of my current situation. Nightmares. Again.

"Oh my lord!" She said while looking at me in distress, "What happened?"

"You are giving me that look. I had a nightmare and it felt so real…the pain was excruciating though…" I said to her.

"No, not that." She stared at me again with that unusual distress that she had occasionally, "Did you cut yourself?"

"What? No!"

"Then what happened to your hair?"

"What do you mean?"

"Like, do you feel stifled when you screamed?"

"Yes, a little bit…I felt like…I can't breath, what is your point, dude?"

She led me from her bed to her dresser before I realized I was there. She pointed to the mirror, and I looked in it.

The same thing happened again, my hair were wrapped all around my neck and grew tighter than the last time. I unwrapped them one piece at a time, and those choke marks on my neck were darker than ever. It felt so strange, but I remained calm. Maybe I should be bold and say it won't happen again in case Carly freaks out, but I do not think that would work.

"Tell her." Jason's voice appeared in my head, "Or else I will."

I looked at my wrist and the cuts were all over the place, blood were in the each of the wound but they weren't spliced, nor did those heal by themselves either.

"What is happening?" Carly asked and tried to hide her panicking voice, "Can you please tell me what is going on? I'm scared. Does Cheryl and Caden know anything about this? What happened to you? Are you allergic to my house? How can I explain your situation to my parents? You have to let me know what is going on, Alexia! Is this the first time something like this had happened?"

"Okay okay slow down. I want to tell you but you are not making this easier for me." She looked at me innocently and I sighed, "Fine, but if I'm telling you this, promise me you're not going to faint?"

"I promise." She said solemnly, "Can't believe I'm not the first one to know about this. Just let me have an idea and I promise nothing will change between us."

"Okay…what if I'm really old…"

"As in…you're married?" She squeezed her eyes together, "Like one of those woman who go undercover as a high school student to get information? Do you work with the FBI?"

"No..Jesus." I looked at her in disbelief.

She titled her eyebrows, "Say what now,

girl? Spill the tea."

"I...I don't know how to tell you this, but only did myself know a couple weeks ago that..." I paused and she still looked confused, "I'm an immortal."

She frowned and bursted out laugher, "I'm assuming you are joking..."

"No, I'm not. Caden and Cheryl all knew about this. I.O stood for immortal organization. Caden is 175 years old and Cheryl is about 220. As for me, I only know I'm even older than Cheryl. I'm not sure about my genetics or heritage either since Caden mentioned something about Italy and I'm from the original family of immortals. Other than that, I'm not so sure about anything else either but I still have a human diet, and I don't die easily nor can be staked."

She gazed at me again, emotionless, "I need a minute."

"Take your time."

She sat on the floor in silence, leaving me watching my arm cuts to heal slowly, "Do you drink blood?" She asked finally.

"No, do you see me drinking?" I laughed.

"Who else knows?"

"Cheryl, Caden, all of the people in I.O, you and probably Jason..."

"Jason?"

"Caden's planning to tell him."

She frowned, "You will have to give me some time to process it. I don't know...it just seems absurd." She grabbed a pointy pencil from her desk and threw it at my face. I grabbed her hand and snatched it without looking at her.

"Still no vampire, don't ever do that again. And don't even think Caden as Ian Somerhalder."

She gave me a grin, "I mean…"

"Nope."

"Fine." She looked disappointed, "Should I call Cheryl though? I'm still worried…and you wouldn't wake up from the dreams no matter how hard I shook you. I can only soak you in water and that worked. Sorry about the cold, I know it gives you chills."

I sighed, "No worries. But don't do it again. And don't call Cheryl, I don't want to worry her. She got a lot on her plate right now and plus, they are having a cocktail party at I.O, I don't want to disturb her."

"Holiday dinner?"

"More like a…science fair, but who cares, let her have her fun."

"Why didn't you go?"

"Caden's parents are the boss of I.O. According to Caden is, 'you can meet my parents any time when you are ready'. So no, not yet. And I don't like all those Dr. Xavier and Dr. Kiki's schizophrenic training monkeys."

"Training monkeys?" Her eyes widened, but then she laughed, "I would never understand you immortals. Gimme some time to go over this whole immortal stuff, okay?"

Her phone rang, "Hello? Yes, this is her. Sure." She walked out of the room while trying to tell me she got to take this, "Yes, okay, okay, okay, sure. I promise. Yes."

"Who was that?" I asked her when she came back.

"Umm…just Jason." She smirked like one of those diabolical stewards that we've seen in movies and I stared, "There's no shenanigans, no espionage or any subterfuge afoot."

I know that look. Something's happening and she wouldn't tell me. It was just like the time when she got sunburn but she told me she thought she got skin cancer since she would not put on any sunscreen and refused to see her family doctor.

"YOU LYING LITTLE WEASEL!"

# ABOUT THE AUTHOR

Yijia Linda Lin is currently a 17-year-old junior at Culver Academies in Culver, IN, United States. She is a published author, a singer, an actress, and an athlete. She enjoys public speaking and western riding. Her first novel, *The Isle* was published in 2020. In addition, her proses, flash fictions, personal narratives, and poetry, such as *Girls Don't Cry*, *A trip to the stars*, *@3 - insomnia*, *my 6 mistakes*, *Carpe Diem* etc. has been featured in various literary magazines worldwide and has won top tier writing contests. She has also released three solo albums and eight collections and has performed on various CCTV channels back home.

www.ingramcontent.com/pod-product-compliance
Lightning Source LLC
Chambersburg PA
CBHW031325130726
47988CB00007B/2987